Art
and
Abuse

DESHAUNA DAVIS

ISBN: 978-1-61244-790-2
Library of Congress Control Number: 2019915652

Printed in the United States of America

Halo Publishing International
1100 NW Loop 410
Suite 700 - 176
San Antonio, Texas 78213
www.halopublishing.com
contact@halopublishing.com

Acknowledgments

When I first started this novel, I didn't expect myself to come this far in my life. And now here I am, a published author. And I couldn't have done it without the help of these special people.

I want to thank my mom, Janel. You were the most supportive when I first started writing this book and, after Dad died, you still pushed me forward. I'm grateful for that. I love you.

I also want to thank my Grandma Agnus and Erika Smith, two people who have supported me since the moment I told the entire family that I wanted to be an author. I love both of you so much, and I can't thank you enough.

To my friend Savannah: When you showed me that character chart, you gave me the idea of writing my novel. And you have no idea how much I appreciate that. You're a great friend and I thank you.

Finally, I want to thank the teachers who have helped me get this far with my novel. Ashland Pingue, my first AVID teacher: You were the first person who believed in me when I told you I wanted to write a book. You helped me with my punctuation, grammar, and the detail of the story. I love you so much.

Next, Ali Goljahmofrad. When I first came to talk with you about my novel, you thought I was like the rest of the other students who came to you about writing a book. But then you saw how serious I am about this story, and you started to believe in me, and I want you to know that I appreciate all the help you've given me.

And, last but not least, Terri Real: When Mr. Goljahmofrad and I came to you about formatting my novel, he told you that I was very committed to this book. Even though you were busy with yearbook production, you still took your time to help me format the story. And I am grateful to you.

Writing a novel is not easy, but with the encouragement of these influential people, I was able to finish this novel and accomplish my dream.

Contents

Chapter 1

ALESEA

After a night of restless sleep, my alarm rang. I got out of bed and did a few stretches; after that, I made my way to the bathroom for a nice, hot shower. Instead of flat-ironing my hair, I decided to keep my natural curls. When I finished drying my hair, I looked at myself in the mirror to see if he had left any hickeys. Lucky for me, he hadn't. I went to my closet to put on some dark blue jeans, a dark red shirt, and a short-sleeved jean jacket. After getting dressed, I surveyed my room. Looking at my nearly-finished artwork, I thought, *Time to show off my art skills.*

I looked around the house to see if anyone was up; thank goodness nobody was. I went to the kitchen and grabbed some muffin batter, blueberries, strawberries, and raspberries. I heard footsteps coming down the stairs. My body started shaking, thinking it was him.

"Good morning, Alesea," a sweet voice greeted. It was my adoptive mother, Aaliyah; one of the most famous fashion designers in California.

"Good morning, Mom."

You're wondering how I got adopted? Well, when I was around like four or five, my parents died in a fire. I didn't have much family around, so I was sent to foster care. My foster mother didn't treat me like the other kids. Everyone bullied me because of how I dressed. I'm an artist; I like wearing shadowy outfits—dark blue, dark red, violet, and dark pink. After months of going through hell, I was taken in by Emory and Aaliyah Macknight.

"So, how's the new painting coming along?" she asked.

"It's going great. I might be able to get someone to pay a pretty good price for it."

"Well, I hope you'll let me be your first buyer, Alesea," a voice piped in.

When I took the muffins out of the oven, I felt his presence behind me: Emory Macknight. Emory, my adoptive father. I've called him by his first name ever since I turned sixteen.

A few years ago, around my sixteenth birthday, Emory came into my room, closing the door slowly as if a baby was sleeping across from me. His eyes were usually bright, but, for some reason, they were dark that night.

"Yeah, Dad?"

"You've grown to be a beautiful young lady, Alesea," he said.

"Thanks, Dad."

He then walked over to me. "And I love beautiful young women."

I felt his hand stroke my arm. He was acting very strange. Then, he did the unspeakable: He kissed me. I was so shocked, I pushed him off me, but he wasn't holding back. He kept kissing me and forced me onto my bed. I was so scared of what he was going to do. I thought he loved me as his own, but I guess I was wrong. Because of him, I became the silent freak of my school and I had no more friends.

I cleared my throat and grabbed a muffin.

"Well, I'm off to school."

"I can drive you if you want, sweetie," Emory said.

I did not want to be alone with this perv. "N-no, thank you. I'm fine," I stuttered as I made my way to the garage.

Chapter 2

On my way to school, I decided to get my usual at Starbucks: coffee with cream and two packets of sugar. When I arrived at school, I noticed that someone was waiting by the school door with their arms and legs crossed. Looking closely, I realized that it was Phoenix Lazaro. Phoenix Lazaro was known as one of the most attractive boys at this school. I had heard rumors that he sold drugs, but I ignored them. I exited my car and walked towards the entrance.

"Hey, babe," greeted Phoenix.

I ignored his comment and headed for my first period. Right before I could open the door, Phoenix opened it for me: "Ladies first."

I walked into the building and whispered: "Thank you."

I entered my first-period class: Art. Looking at the board, our assignment that day was to sketch something with a number-two pencil. I went over to my seat, took out my sketchbook, and started drawing. Every time I do my work, I ignore everything around me.

Someone touched my shoulder and I smacked their hand.

"Sorry, I didn't mean to scare you."

The voice belonged to someone I didn't recognize. I may not talk to a lot of people here, but that doesn't mean I don't know their names. "No, I'm sorry. I didn't hear you come in."

This new kid looked pretty cool. He had short, wavy, ginger hair; blue eyes; and a beautiful jawline. He extended his hand to me. "I'm Jason, Jason King." He seemed nice, but I don't trust people that easily.

"Alesea, Alesea Macknight." It quickly got awkward in the room.

"So, uh, does anyone sit here?" he asked me, pointing at the seat next to me. I shook my head no, and he took the chair.

Thirty minutes later, the bell rang for second period. I packed up my things and turned in my assignment.

Entering the hallway, I heard footsteps catching up with me.

"Hey, Alesea!" Jason called out. I turned to him. "Hey, you seem nice. Maybe you can show me around?"

I had never thought of showing around a new kid. But, since I'm the top honor roll student here, I might as well. I was about to answer his request when an awful stench entered my nostrils.

"Hey, handsome." I knew that voice very well. Marissa Johnson.

Marissa Johnson, known as the most popular girl in school. She's had a ton of guys around her, but she only has eyes for Phoenix. She's liked him ever since middle school. They've never talked, but they both went to the same school. We don't ever get along—apparently she's jealous of me because I'm at the top of everything and because some of the hot guys try to ask me out.

"Wouldn't you rather I show you around, instead of this weirdo?" she asked, batting her fake eyelashes.

I didn't want to start my morning with her. I was about to leave, but Jason got the last word: "Thank you, but no, thank you."

He gently took my hand in his. "I'd rather this weirdo show me around than be seen with a fake person like you." Jason started pulling me away from a pissed-off Marissa. Once we were far away from her, I took my hand out of Jason's.

"Sorry about that," he said.

I let out an annoyed sigh. *This is not a good day for me*, I told myself. "You still want me to show you around?" I asked, still a little annoyed.

He nodded his head. "Yeah." I started to walk, with Jason following me.

Chapter 3

I showed Jason the whole school: the gym, the cafeteria, the library (my favorite spot), the chemistry lab, the computer lab, and the rooftop garden. After our tour, it was time for lunch. When we entered the cafeteria, I got chicken tetrazzini, while Jason got the homemade chili.

Most of the tables were taken, except my favorite spot with a perfect view of the city. I took my seat next to the window, and Jason sat across from me.

"Thanks for the tour, Alesea. This school is pretty great."

I nodded. Lunch was going fine until I heard two other chairs creak against the floor: my acquaintances, Bernadet Fetsku and her best friend Maeve Kaja. I'd talked to them a few times, but only during group projects.

"Hi, Alesea," Bernadet greeted cheerfully.

"Hey, Bernadet." I wasn't really in the mood for a lively talk.

"Bernadet, leave her alone, you know she's not in a cheerful mood," Maeve said. She knew when I didn't want to be bothered.

"Are you friends of Alesea?" asked Jason.

"We're more like acquaintances," said Bernadet. "We've been trying to become her friends, but she's a tough cookie."

I laughed at her little joke.

"She'll open up to us when she's ready," said Maeve. I knew these guys were trying hard to be my friends, but I didn't know if I could trust them.

Lunch was almost over. I was starting to enjoy Jason, Bernadet, and Maeve.

"Don't look now, but Mr. and Mrs. Popular just walked in," Maeve said.

I looked up and saw Marissa and her posse with Phoenix and his group. When Marissa caught me staring at Phoenix, she gave me a death glare, but it didn't affect me. Then Phoenix caught my gaze, too. He smiled at me and gave me a sexy wink. I felt my cheeks starting to burn, so I finished my tetrazzini and exited the cafeteria.

While I was walking through the hallway, I heard footsteps behind me. I let out an annoyed sigh: "What do you want?"

Turning around, I saw that Phoenix had his usual cocky smile. "I just want to talk, babe."

I rolled my eyes at him. "First of all, I'm not your babe. And secondly, shouldn't you be with your girlfriend?"

He started laughing at me, which made me more annoyed with him. "She's not my girlfriend. She's just another side chick."

"Of course she is."

I was about to walk away when I felt his hand pull me into his chest. I looked into his eyes, and he asked, "Tell me, Alesea, what do I have to do to make you mine?"

When he asked me that question, I knew what he wanted. So, I gave him a mischievous smile and then kicked him where the sun doesn't shine. He fell on the floor holding his cock, groaning in pain.

"You can leave me the hell alone because I will never go out with a player like you."

I left him there, on the ground, in pain. I didn't need a man in my life.

Chapter 4

PHOENIX

I was looking at my laptop with an ice pack on my crotch. Someone knocked on my door. My bro Geo came in.

"What is it, Geo?"

He planted another ice pack on my desk. "Thought you might need another one."

I looked at the bag. "Peas?"

He shrugged his shoulders. "It was the only one you had left." I shrugged and switched out the ice pack for the peas. "I didn't expect her to kick you in the nuts, dude."

I let out an exhausted sigh. "Yeah, well, neither did I."

Geo smiled smugly. "So, you want to call it quits?"

Geo and I had made a bet: If I slept with Alesea, he would have to give up his baby, his 2019 Kia Forte.

"Not a chance. I'm going to win, for sure."

"Whatever you say, Phoenix."

I knew Alesea was going to be at the art festival, so that might be my chance. I was going to have to pull the nice guy routine.

Chapter 5

ALESEA

After having kicked Phoenix in the balls and waiting through hours of school, I finally got home to my masterpiece. I let out a relieved sigh—*Finally, it's finished*, I thought—but my body started to shake. I felt a presence behind me.

"Wow, Alesea, you've outdone yourself."

"T-thank you, E-Emory."

He wrapped his arms around my waist, pulling me close to his chest. "I believe you deserve a reward." He started kissing my neck. I felt shivers go down my spine. I started choking on tears.

"Please, not now," I begged.

"That's not your decision, Alesea."

And, right then and there, he raped me again.

When he finished, I heard Aaliyah's voice: "Emory."

"Yes, dear?"

"You'd better get going, or you'll miss seeing the other artwork."

"We're on our way."

He exited my room, and Aaliyah came in. She walked towards me.

"Alesea?" She put her hand on my shoulder. "Is there something you want to tell me?" I knew that that question was coming soon, but I also knew what would happen if I said anything.

September 15, 2019: Aaliyah was gone for a few weeks. I was in my room, letting Emory do his thing. When he finished, he walked over to me and whispered, "If you ever tell your mother about this, then I will send you back to that foster care. And you don't want that, now, do you?" A small tear rolled down my cheek; I shook my head. "That's a good girl." He kissed my forehead and left me in solitude.

"No, Mom. Nothing's wrong."

I grabbed my paintings and went to the car. I set my artwork down and opened the trunk. I was about to put in my canvases when I felt a hand rub my ass. I was about to drop my work, but his hand covered my mouth. His mouth came close to my ear.

"You didn't tell Aaliyah, did you?" I shook my head very slow; I didn't want to get him mad. "That's a good girl. Now, close the trunk and get in the car."

Arriving back at school, Emory helped me set up my art stand. Looking around, I saw that a lot of people loved art. Next thing I knew, Jason, Bernadet, and Maeve were coming my way.

"Wow, Alesea. Your paintings are amazing," Jason said.

I smiled a little. "Thanks, Jason. So, what are you guys looking for?" I let them look at my work.

"I'll take the one with the moon shining in the ocean," Maeve said.

"That will be five bucks."

She took out her black velvet wallet and gave me five dollars. I took the painting off the shelf and handed it to Maeve. She smiled. "Thanks, Alesea."

I smiled back at her. "No problem, Maeve." I looked at Bernadet and Jason, "So, any other requests?"

After that, Jason left with my "all alone" painting. It depicts a girl in the middle of the ocean, looking at her reflection. And Bernadet took my werewolf painting— a young girl getting bitten by her werewolf boyfriend. I was now down to three canvases: my red moon painting, the magical red rose, and a broken heart.

"Wow. I must say, young lady, you have some talent."

My face was in shock. My eyes widened, and my mouth was open. I turned around and saw: "Johnson Knight!"

He showed me his entirely white, shiny teeth. "In the flesh, my dear. And, might I say, you have an eye for art."

OMG. I just got complimented by my ideal. I tried not to say it out loud. "Thank you, sir." I showed him the rest of my paintings. "So, do any of them interest you?"

He put his fingers under his chin. "I'll take the broken heart one, with blood slowly slipping out of it."

I gave him a genuine smile. That had been my first painting.

Mr. Knight left with what he called a "masterpiece," and he paid me with a check for a thousand dollars. I put the check in my back pocket and then heard another set of feet approach my stand. I put on a smile, but it turned into a frown when I saw his face.

"Hey Alesea," Phoenix greeted awkwardly.

"Phoenix."

Things got quiet quickly. "Wow, so these are your paintings?" he asked, looking back at my work.

"Yeah." Turning back to him, I asked, "But you don't want to see Marissa's artwork? I bet she's a better artist than me."

He shook his head. "The only artist I want to see is you," he said with a smile. The way he was talking to me, it made me smile a little.

"Thanks." I felt my cheeks starting to heat up, so I turned my back to him. I cleared my throat. "So, ah, any paintings that capture your interest?

After a few minutes of thinking, Phoenix chose my painting of a random woman in a beautiful wedding dress with white roses. He slid a hundred-dollar bill over to me and smiled, telling me to keep the change. For once in my life, I felt happy around Phoenix. He was about to leave, but he stopped.

"Hey, I'm hosting a Halloween party at my place. Do you want to come?" For the first in my life, someone had invited me to a party. I had always felt like an outcast.

"I don't know?"

He walked back over to my stand, took out a sticky note, and then wrote something on it. He handed me a sticky note. "Think about it."

After Phoenix left, I looked at the sticky note: there were numbers on it. *Phoenix Lazaro gave me his contact information. A lot of girls would be excited to have his digits. Guess I now know how they feel.* I felt someone staring at me. Looking up, I saw Emory's green eyes glaring at me. He was mad.

No, he was enraged.

Emory punished me in the car, and it hurt worse than before. "Is he your boyfriend?" he asked with anger. I couldn't look away from him, so I had to answer.

"No, sir."

"Good, because you know I don't share."

After my punishment, we traveled back home. When we entered the living room, Aaliyah was sitting on the couch with a stranger and two police officers.

"Aaliyah, what's going on?" asked Emory.

A blue-eyed officer looked at Emory. "Emory Macknight?" he asked.

"Yes?"

Emory was starting to get suspicious, and so was I. The officer with blue eyes and a brown-eyed officer walked over to us. The officer with brown eyes took out his handcuffs.

"Emory Macknight, you are under arrest for the rape of your adopted daughter Alesea. You have the right to remain silent. Anything you say can and will be used against you in a court of law."

I couldn't believe my eyes. Emory was getting arrested.

"Whoa, whoa, whoa. You can't arrest me without any proof!"

"They do have proof," Aaliyah said. She walked over to Emory with a file and CD case in her hand. "I had cameras installed all over the house for you. When I saw you go into Alesea's room, I thought you were cheating on me with our daughter. But when I saw you hitting her and stripping her, I was disgusted."

Emory was shocked. He was caught red-handed. "Baby, I . . ."

Aaliyah connected her hand to his face. I was shocked. I'd never seen her mad before.

"How could you do this to our daughter?!" she shouted. "We raised her as our own."

Emory was silent the whole time. There was nothing he could say to stop this.

"Let's go, rapist." The officer with brown eyes handcuffed Emory and took him outside.

I— I didn't know how I felt. I was happy and sad at the same time. Someone put their hand on my shoulder; I turned to see that Aaliyah was looking at me with sad eyes.

"Oh, sweetheart. I'm sorry I didn't do anything to stop him."

I felt the tears come streaming down my face. *"Mom."*

Aaliyah pulled me into an embrace. I don't know how long I was crying on her shoulder, but it felt like hours. I eventually heard someone clear their throat.

"Sorry to interrupt this sad moment, but there's a reason why I'm here, too."

Aaliyah and I separated and went to sit on the couch with the man. He and I shook hands.

"My name is Mark Hemena. I'm a private detective."

Aaliyah turned to me and smiled. "He's been sent to find you, Alesea."

"By who?" I asked. *Who would send a private detective to find me?*

"Your parents," said Mark.

I was surprised. "That's impossible. My parents died in a fire."

Mark shook his head. "No, Alesea, the people who died were your mother's sister and your father's brother."

I was alarmed. "My parents are alive?"

Chapter 6

The day before, I had heard the most ground-shaking news I'd ever gotten: that my parents were alive. I thought, *I just don't get it. It means that the people who raised me for the first four years of my life were my aunt and uncle. If my birth parents are looking for me, then I want to meet them.*

"Hey, Alesea, want to have sex?"

I wish. Wait . . .

"What?"

Oh, right. I was having lunch with Bernadet, Maeve, and Jason. I must've dozed off.

"Well, that got her attention. Thanks, Phoenix," said Maeve.

I turned around and saw Phoenix standing next to me. So, he's the one who asked that question.

"Hey, gorgeous, mind if I sit?" he asked.

Why did the most popular bad boy in school want to sit at my table? He must be high or something.

"I don't think she wants you here. Besides, none of us want to deal with your side-piece right now. I know I don't," said Maeve.

She was right. I had a lot on my mind and I didn't want to deal with Phoenix's flirtation.

"I believe that's Alesea's decision." I let out an annoyed sigh and gave Phoenix a death glare. He held up his hands in defeat. "Okay, I get it, but I hope you'll be at the party next week."

He left our table and went back to his posse. *What's with him? He was all nice to me at the art festival, now he's acting like a player again.*

"Wait, when did he invite you to his party?" Jason asked.

"Yesterday, at the art festival. He was being nice to me and just asked me." I shrugged my shoulders. "But I don't think I'm going to go."

"We'll go with you if it makes you feel better," offered Bernadet.

I was surprised. "Really?"

"Of course," she said.

I smiled at them. They'd been helpful to me ever since I had felt like opening up.

"All right, I'll go." Bernadet smiled at me, as did Maeve and Jason.

"Great! So, next week we can go shopping at Party City."

I liked that idea, going shopping.

The week went by fast, and soon it was the night of Phoenix's party. We arrived at Party City and saw Halloween decorations hanging all over.

"Okay, let's meet back at the register in fifteen minutes," said Bernadet.

We all separated and looked for our costumes. The women's clothing options seemed a little too showy for my body. *Wait a minute. Why buy an outfit when I have a mother who's a famous fashion designer?* I looked around the store and found Bernadet. When I saw her, she was looking at sexy costumes.

"Hey, Bernadet, I'm going to go."

"What? Why? We just got here." She was confused.

"I forgot that I have a mother who's the number-one fashion designer," I explained.

"Oh, right."

I left the store and went home. When I got back, I noticed how quiet it was, then I remembered that Emory was in jail. It felt nice. I went up to Aaliyah's office and saw her using her sewing machine.

She finally noticed me: "Oh, hi, honey," she greeted. "So, did you find a costume?"

I started playing with my fingers. "Um, that's what I wanted to talk to you about, Mom." I was about to ask her, but she held up her hand before I can speak.

"You don't have to ask. I have one question." She gave me a broad, girly smile. "What do you want to be?"

I had already thought about what I wanted to be, but now I wanted something different. "I want to be a mysterious genie, with a veil covering my mouth and a top that doesn't show that much skin."

Aaliyah nodded her head, understanding. "Okay, just give me an hour and a half, and then I'll do your makeup."

I smiled, "Okay, Mom." I left her office and let her do her magic.

While I was waiting for my costume, I was just laying on my bed and sketching. My phone beeped. I looked at the screen. It was a text from Bernadet: *Hey, we all chose our costumes. We'll be at your place in twenty minutes.*

I texted her back: *K. Aaliyah's almost done making mine.*

Within a few seconds, she texted, *Great, can't wait to see it. :)*

When I put my phone back on my bed, there was a knock on my door—"Come in."

My door opened and Aaliyah came in, holding my costume. Its top covered most of my stomach, the bottoms and sleeves were silky, and she had used my favorite color, dark red.

"Mom, it's beautiful." I put on my costume and then Aaliyah did my makeup.

Ten minutes later, when I heard my curling iron touch the countertop, I opened my eyes and saw my reflection. Aaliyah smiled at me and asked, "Well, what do you think?"

Looking at myself, I never thought I could look beautiful again. The black eyeliner was perfect, the eyeshadow was darker than my costume, and the lipstick was a light shade of red.

"It's perfect, Mom."

She smiled at me, holding the veil in her hand. She wrapped it around my mouth. "Now you look perfect," she said.

The doorbell rang before we even left the bathroom. "That must be the others," I said. I exited the bathroom and went to the front door. Opening the door, I saw everyone in their costumes: Jason was Jack Sparrow, Bernadet was a doctor, and Maeve was a policewoman.

When they saw me in my outfit, the girls were more surprised. "Dang, girl. We never thought you would dress sexy," explained Maeve.

"Maeve's right, Alesea. You look gorgeous," complimented Bernadet.

"Thanks, guys."

Jason cleared his throat, capturing our attention. "So, are you ladies ready to go, or what?"

We all laughed at his comment. "Yes, Jason, we're going." We left my house and headed straight for Phoenix's place.

Chapter 7

When we finally arrived at Phoenix's apartment complex, we saw that there was a long line.

"Do we have to wait in that long line?" asked Maeve.

"Nah, I think if I tell the guard my name, he'll let us in."

We got out of Jason's car and went over to the guard. People were shouting at us for cutting the line. When we got to the front of the line, the guard looked at us. "Names?" he asked.

"My name's Alesea Macknight. These are my friends Bernadet Fetsku, Maeve Kaja, and Jason King."

He looked at the list. "Oh, yeah, you're on here, and the boss figured you'd bring your friends." He unclipped the rope. "Go on in."

I nodded my head and entered the building. I pressed the button for the tenth floor, the doors closed, and we went up.

What we saw when we arrived was a ton of people in costumes, girls twerking, and others drinking.

"Wow, the dude may be a douche, but he sure knows how to throw a party," said Maeve.

I started to feel very uncomfortable. "I feel like I don't belong here."

I felt a hand on my shoulder. "Don't worry, Alesea, just stick with us," Bernadet said.

Surprisingly, I was having a blast at this party. I was getting compliments from guys, even the popular ones. I had gone back to the bar to get a soda when I felt a tap my shoulder. I turned and saw Phoenix, dressed like a member of a SWAT team.

"Well, well, well, aren't you a pretty genie."

Even though I was having fun, I was still not in the mood to see him. "Yes, and this genie has no desire in granting *you* wishes."

He showed his usual smile. "I like 'em sassy." I rolled my eyes, and then Marissa came over and grabbed Phoenix's arm.

"Phoenix, babe, come dance with me." She pulled him to the dance floor before giving me a death glare.

Back with my group, we were all dancing but, for some reason, I started feeling dizzy.

"You okay, Alesea?" asked Maeve.

"I'm . . . good," I tried to explain, but then everything went black.

****

PHOENIX

My party was going perfectly. I had a scotch in my right hand and a blunt in the other. My homeboy, Geo, sat on the other side of the couch.

"We need to talk."

"What is it?" I asked, looking confused.

"Okay, so, while you were talking to Alesea earlier, I put ethanol in her soda. I told her friends to take her to your room. So this is your chance to take her."

"What?!" I smacked him in the head. "You, idiot, that's not how I want to do this!" I wanted to have sex with Alesea, not rape her.

"I'm sorry. I was trying to help."

"Yeah, well, you're not."

I went upstairs and headed for my room. When I made it there, I noticed that the door was slightly open. I peeked inside and saw my men putting their hands on Alesea. Busting through the door, they were all shocked to see me.

"What the fuck are y'all doing?!"

"Oh, hey, boss. Care to join us?" asked Nix, my sniper.

Okay, now I was pissed. Alesea then punched him in the face. She ran towards me and hid behind me; I could feel her shaking.

"You okay?" I asked. She nodded, still shaking. I grabbed her head and whispered, "Wait outside." She didn't think twice about my order.

I glared at these idiots. "What the hell is wrong with you, dumbasscs?!"

"Come on, boss. We were about to have some fun. You could've joined us," said Ivo, my drug holder.

I don't know how they knew about this bet, but I knew one thing: They needed to pay the price.

****

ALESEA

I waited outside of Phoenix's room after those three goons tried to touch me. I don't know what happened before that. All I remembered was that my friends had brought me to this room. When those goons came in and started touching me, I didn't know I was crying until I felt tears running down my face.

The door opened and Phoenix came out, asking, "Everything all right?" I nodded. He took my hand and told me, "I'll take you home." He led me to the garage and we got into his 2019 Buggati Veyron.

The drive to my house was tranquil. I was staring out the window until Phoenix broke the silence.

"Did they rape you?"

I shook my head.

"Well, the good news is, you're still a virgin."

I stayed quiet after he made that comment.

When we finally arrived at my house, he offered to walk me to the front porch.

"Get some rest. You'll feel better in the morning."

He was about to walk back to his car when I said, "Hey." He stopped and automatically my arms wrapped around him. "Thanks for saving me."

I felt his left hand on my back, and the other gently stroking my hair. "You're welcome."

I walked back to the front door and waved to Phoenix.

Chapter 8

It was mid-November and I was sitting at the table, eating dinner with Aaliyah. Every time I tried to eat, my eyes went back to her. She sighed.

"All right, Alesea. Spit it out. You've been staring at me since we sat down."

I cleared my throat. "Um, Aaliyah, I've thought that, for Thanksgiving, I want to meet my parents."

Her face showed how surprised she was. "Are you sure, honey? Are you positive that's what you want?" I nodded. "All right, baby, go pack your stuff. We'll leave tomorrow morning."

I scratched my neck a little. "Um, actually, Mom, I was thinking of going by myself."

She let out a sigh. "Okay, Alesea, I respect your decision."

I got up from the table and hugged her tightly. "Thanks for raising me, Mom."

Her arms tightened around me. "Thanks for being the best daughter I can ask for."

After dinner, I packed my clothes.

The next morning, I asked the private detective for my family's address. It turned out that my mom and dad live in Magnolia, Texas. Aaliyah offered to let me use the private jet, but I refused. I purchased the first ticket to Texas that I could find. The flight was three hours long, so I just drew.

When the plane landed, I went to Starbucks and ordered my original. I called a cab, asking him to take me to 127 Whispering Meadow, Magnolia, Montgomery County, Texas. Once we arrived, we saw a large gate, and two guards were blocking the path. The guard on the left approached the car.

"Can I help you, miss?"

This guy was a little scary. By the looks of his muscles, he could break anyone in one snap of a finger.

"I—I'm here t-to see Hayden and M-Madison C-Croft."

He raised his left eyebrow at me. "Why do you need to see my bosses?"

I took a deep breath. "My name is Alesea Allyse Malerie Macknight. I am the long lost daughter of Mr. and Mrs. Croft."

He looked at the other guard and nodded. The gate started to open; the driver took off.

We arrived at the entrance and, looking at the house, I was mesmerized. The home was so beautiful. I wondered how my life would be if I lived here. I rang the doorbell but after a few minutes no one had answered. After another minute, a maid answered the door.

She smiled, asking, "Can I help you, ma'am?"

"Are Mr. and Mrs. Croft in?"

She nodded, "Oh yes, they're in their office. But Mr. Croft might be in a little mood. Follow me, please?"

We went upstairs and stopped at a set of white double doors. The maid faced me. "Please wait here." I waited outside, swaying back and forth. The door opened and the maid came out, telling me, "They'll see you now."

I took a deep breath. *Here we go*.

I entered the office. All I saw were pictures of Hayden, Madison, a toddler, and a baby. Everything in the office looked expensive. "Can we help you, miss?" a male voice asked. I turned and saw the man and woman who claimed to be my mother and father. Their faces were shocked when they saw me.

"A-Alesea?" asked Madison.

"H-hi, Mom, Dad."

My father got up and walked over to me. He put his hands on my face and smiled at me. I smiled back and, the next thing I knew, he had pulled me close, into his chest.

"My little girl."

The tears came out, and I didn't care. "Dad."

Another pair of arms tightens the hold. "We missed you, sweetie," Madison said.

The moment was interrupted when someone knocked on the door.

"Enter," my father said.

A young man who looked like my father entered the room. "Hey, Dad . . ." He saw mom and dad hugging me.

Hayden cleared his throat. "Xavier, you remember your sister Alesea?"

The man known as my brother, Xavier, walked over to me. Madison and Hayden gave us some space. Xavier took hold of my hands, looked deeply into my eyes. "I never forgot." He pulled me close.

"Xavier, take Alesea to the living room. We'll explain everything later," said Madison. Xavier nodded then led me out of the office.

We got to the living room and waited for Hayden and Madison. I heard their footsteps, and then another pair of feet, coming down the stairs. I saw a little girl hiding behind Hayden's leg.

"It's okay, princess, no need to be shy." The little girl came out from behind Hayden. "Alesea, this is your little sister, Maree. Maree, this is Alesea."

Maree came over, staring at me. I smiled. "Hi, Maree." She kept staring at me until I felt her hug me.

"Hi, Sissy."

I picked her up and hugged her back. Hayden and Madison took a seat on the other side of the couch.

"All right, Alesea, we'll tell you everything. But we need to ask you something—" I held Maree in my lap, waiting for the question. "Do you believe in mobsters?"

Chapter 9

MADISON, 2001

Hayden and I met on a dating website, Text for Love. He's everything I've wanted in a man. He makes a ton of money, he's a sweetheart, loves kids, and he loves strong women. A bunch of my co-workers think I'm getting catfished, but my heart tells me I can trust him.

June 16, 2001: The day we finally got to meet. After I got off work that day, he asked if I wanted to meet face-to-face. I was so thrilled. I scheduled a passport-application appointment. He lived in Texas, while I lived in France. I took time off and planned for the first flight to Texas.

The flight took nearly eleven hours. When the plane landed, I looked around in the crowd at arrivals for a sign with my name. When I finally saw it, I got excited, but who I saw holding that sign wasn't Hayden. The man that stood in front of me kind of looked like

Hayden, but this man had a scar on his right eye. His hair was much darker than Hayden's and he had blue eyes.

"Are you Madison?" he asked.

"Oui."

"My brother couldn't make it, because of the paparazzi, so he asked me to come and get you."

"So, you must be Mikey, Hayden's younger brother."

He smiled and we shook hands. After we retrieved my bags, I noticed that Mikey had been telling the truth about the paparazzi. Outside the airport, reporters were waiting for us.

"Hurry," Mikey said.

We hurried to the limo and the driver opened the door. "Sir," he greeted Mikey and then looked at me, "Mistress."

The drive was long. Finally, when we got there, I saw the house. It was huge. The place was two stories, and the front was fabulous: dark-brown marble, a fountain. We entered the house and Mikey showed me my room.

"Once you're all settled in, I'd love to show you the garden."

I nodded.

"At the entrance, there's a trail of white roses. Follow it," said Mikey.

I followed the petals, wondering where they'd take me. Once the trails of petals stopped, I found myself in the center of a maze. I looked up and saw all my favorite foods: French crullers (twisted, glazed doughnuts with sugar frosting) and French-Canadian meatball stew (a bunch of pork balls and potatoes with flavored gravy and roasted flour).

I thought I heard something, but nobody was around. I started backing up, till my back hit a wall, and then I realized something: Walls don't have eight-packs. Two hands touched my shoulders and a voice tickled my ear.

"Guess who?"

"Hayden!"

I jumped into his arms, and we kissed very passionately.

"Ready to have some fun, love?"

Spending time with Hayden was the most fantastic time of my life. He showed me around Texas, he took me to dinner, showed me the best tour guides and the best malls. Everything was perfect until one night when I found the truth about Hayden.

Three days later he and I were in his room, doing . . . adult things.

"I dreamt of doing this so many times," Hayden said.

I laughed. "You're hopeless, Hayden."

He kissed my forehead, and I cuddled closer to him. The moment ended when his phone rang.

"What?" I heard the other voice from the other end of the line but couldn't make it out. "Are you sure?" he asked. "All right, I'm on my way." He hung up the phone and put on his clothes. "Sorry, dear, something came up at work."

"Will you be back when I wake up?"

He kissed my lips quickly. "I'll be right back." I smiled, and he left me to rest.

After a few hours of sleep, Hayden still hadn't returned. I tried going back to sleep, but I heard a scream. I didn't know whose scream it was. I put on my robe and followed the cry. It led me to a door that I'd never noticed—my guess was the basement. I turned the knob. Walking down the stairs, I saw a light coming from underneath another door. Pushing the door open a bit, I saw a man on the ground, coughing up blood.

Then I heard a familiar voice: "I'll ask again, who hired you to watch the Croft family?" shouted Hayden.

What the hell was going on?

"You should know, bub, that the Croft family is the strongest mob family in America," explained Mikey.

What?! Hayden's a mobster. He lied to me, from the beginning of our relationship.

"End him. He's not going to talk," ordered Hayden.

"Sure, bro," said Mikey.

A gun fired, but I covered my eyes.

"Call someone to clean up this mess. I have to get back to Madison."

"Sure, Hayden."

Footsteps were coming close to the door. I tried running to the stairs, but I was too late.

"Madison?!" There he was. The man I supposedly loved was staring at me with a shocked face. "H-how much did you hear?" he asked.

I ran as fast as I could back to my room. I heard Hayden's footsteps following me. I made it to my room and tried to close the door, but his foot was blocking it.

"Let me in, Madison," he ordered

"Leave me alone, Hayden!"

"Madison if you don't open this door in the next ten seconds, I'll force it open."

I didn't want to risk it, so I opened the door.

"Can we please talk about what you heard?" he asked.

We sat down and talked about his family business. It turns out that his family had been mobsters ever since his great-great-grandfather met his great-great-grandmother. His mother's side is half-American and half-Japanese. And since he's firstborn, he'll have to take over the business and become the boss of the mob. And when he saw my dating profile, he thought I'd make the perfect mob wife.

"Hayden, I don't think this is going to work."

"A-are you breaking up with me?!"

I nodded. "I do love you, Hayden, but I don't think I'm cut out to be a mob wife."

He let out a sigh and held my face. "Then I want you to remember who loved you more." He pressed his lips onto mine and kissed me possessively.

It was early in the morning by then, so I purchased the earliest available flight to Paris, France. Before I left, I gave Hayden a goodbye kiss. The trip back home was depressing: I had just found out what my (now ex-) boyfriend did for a living, and now we might never see each other again.

Three weeks after I got back to Paris, I started feeling sick, nauseous, and having weird cravings. So, I went to the doctor for a checkup.

I was surprised by what the doctor then told me: "Congratulations, Ms. Cooler. You're expecting."

I was three weeks pregnant.

Chapter 10

HAYDEN

March 16, 2002: Nine months since Madison dumped me and I'd been in a bad mood ever since she left me. She stopped answering my texts, she stopped posting things on Facebook, and she won't answer my calls. So I hired a private detective to look after her.

What shocked me the most was the picture of her and her big belly. She was carrying my child. I knew that I had to see her again. I scheduled a private flight to France and made sure to buy some presents for my son or daughter.

After hours of thinking about what I was going to say to Madison, the plane finally landed in France. I hired a limo driver to take me to her apartment complex. When I arrived, I saw movers moving boxes into a van and then I saw Madison, walking out of the building with another woman. I guessed it was her sister or friend. When they saw the limo, I told the driver to stay out of sight, but I made sure that I could still see Madison.

I saw her go inside the complex, so I followed her into the elevator. She was shocked to see me.

"Hello, Madison."

She looked at me with fear in her, like I was going to hurt her. I looked at her stomach. I got down on both knees and put my ear on her belly. Very gently, I rubbed her stomach and felt a bump on my hand. I smiled. "Why didn't you tell me?" She was about to talk, but she closed her mouth. I got up from my knees and held her close. "It's okay, we can talk about it later."

After all, her stuff was packed. We moved her things into her new house. It was lovely, a one-story house with a big backyard, two bedrooms, and two bathrooms. I helped her unpack her stuff and bring in the gifts from her baby shower. It turns out that we were having a boy. She was going to name him Xavier.

"Hayden?" Madison asked.

"Yeah?"

"I didn't tell you about Xavier because I want him to have a normal childhood instead of being in the mafia."

I understood her decision for our son. I, too, wanted him to have a normal childhood before I told him about our family business.

"Madison, I understand your decision. Once he's born and grows older, then we'll tell him about the mob." She smiled and leaned on my shoulder. I finally felt like I was at peace. Then I felt something wet on my shoes. I looked at Madison and she was in shock. "It's time?"

She looked me straight in the eyes, smiling. "It's time."

****

MADISON, FIVE YEARS LATER

Holding my baby girl in my arms, I saw she had my hair and her father's skin. Alesea was so beautiful. There was a knock on the door. My husband Hayden and our five-year-old son Xavier entered.

"Hi, honey," Hayden greeted.

"Hi, Mommy," Xavier greeted.

"Hi, boys." They came closer to the bed, looking at Alesea and me. "Say hi to your baby sister, Xavier."

Hayden picked him up and put him on the bed. He gently touched Alesea's hand, and she grabbed his finger. He smiled at her. There was another knock.

"Who is it?" asked Hayden.

"It's Mikey."

"Come in."

Mikey and his girlfriend Allie entered the room.

"So, this is Alesea?" he asked.

"Yep. Isn't she beautiful?" asked Hayden.

"Yeah. Yeah, she is."

I looked at my son, who had a sad look on his face.

"Uncle Mikey, do you have to take Alesea away?"

Mikey looked at Xavier and patted his head. "Don't worry, bud. She'll be safe with us." He held out his pinky. "I pinky promise."

Xavier smiled and linked his pinky with Mikey's.

****

ALESEA

"And that's how your life began to change, Alesea," Hayden said.

"H-how did the fire happen?" I asked.

"Our rivals found out your location and decided to start a fire," explained Madison.

"Did you ever find out who killed them?"

"It was the Irish mafia. They wanted revenge against us."

Xavier took my hand in his. "Don't worry, Sis. We'll get them," he said.

I hoped they would.

Chapter 11

Thanksgiving week with my parents was fantastic. I met the rest of my family, from both of my parents' sides. They were all excited to finally get to meet me. Then I got to know my siblings: Xavier was an amazing big brother to Maree, and he taught me how to defend myself since I've been thinking about getting a gun for protection.

Now I was back home and ready for my life to go back to normal.

The next morning at school, I was retrieving my books out of my locker when I heard, "Hey, Alesea."

It was Ryan Saxfield, the second-most popular guy in high school. He was like a magnet to all the girls but, for some reason, he always had an eye on me. I don't know why.

"Hi, Ryan." I started walking with Ryan beside me. I looked at him and saw him smiling at me. "Do you need something?" I asked him.

"I was wondering if you wanted to go on a date with me?"

I stopped right at my classroom, completely confused. "Excuse me?"

"A date. You and me. The art gallery, dinner, and a nice walk on the boardwalk."

Ryan Saxfield is asking me out.

"I-I . . . don't know, Ryan."

"Come on, what's wrong with going on a date with me?" he asked.

I shrugged my shoulders. "All right."

He smiled. "Great. Pick you up at eight."

After school, I killed some time by going through my closet for my date with Ryan. I knew I shouldn't feel excited about going out, but for some reason I did. When I finally found something suitable for the night, I put on a little bit of makeup.

"Alesea, some handsome man is here for you," shouted Aaliyah.

How embarrassing.

"Thank you, Ms. Macknight," said Ryan.

"Please, call me Aaliyah."

She left the two of us alone.

"I like the different colors on your shirt—very creative."

I was wearing a mixed T-shirt, with violet, dark blue, and light ocean blue.

"Thanks."

He held his arm out to me. "Ready to go?"

I took his arm. "Ready as I'll ever be."

As it turned out, the date with Ryan wasn't as bad as I thought. It was charming. We had dinner at a very fancy Italian restaurant called Marco's Palazzo, he took me to my favorite art museum, and we walked on the sandy beach. It was the best night of my life. We drove back to my house while he told a few jokes.

He walked me to my doorstep. "Okay, I'll admit that was the best first date I've ever had. Thanks, Ryan."

He smiled. "It was my pleasure."

We just stared at each other for a little bit, then he got closer to me and leaned towards my lips. Our lips connected, and it felt nice. We pulled apart and Ryan told me goodnight. And I knew that my life was lightening up.

Chapter 12

After my date with Ryan, we started dating. He was charming; even my friends loved him. He treated me like a princess and he wasn't like most guys, wanting girls for their bodies.

The next day, at school, I was walking to the cafeteria when, suddenly, someone pulled me into the janitor's closet. Once I was inside, Phoenix was glaring at me.

"What's going on with you and Saxfield?"

His voice was calm, but I could see the fire in his eyes. I crossed my arms. "What Ryan and I are doing is none of your business."

He got closer to me, and my back hit the wall. "Are you sleeping with him?"

I gasped, "I can't believe you think I'm a whore."

I tried to leave, but he pulled me back to the wall and smiled at me wickedly. "Where do you think you're going, Alesea?"

I was surprised by his next move: He smashed his lips onto mine. I tried to break free of his grip, but the way he did things with his mouth was incredible. Soon I just gave in and kissed him back. He picked me up, I wrapped my legs around him. We were then interrupted, but we didn't care.

"Alesea?!"

We stopped kissing and saw Ryan looking shocked. Then his emotions changed into anger. He pulled Phoenix off me, dragged me out of the closet, he kept pulling my wrist until we were far away from Phoenix.

"Ryan, you're hurting me."

We finally stopped walking. He faced me. "I never want to see him around again."

The look on his face showed that he wasn't joking.

"Okay, I'll try."

He then grabbed both of my shoulders. "Don't try, Alesea. You do."

What was happening? This wasn't the Ryan I knew; this was a different person.

"I-I got to go."

I escaped from his grip and ran as fast as I could. "Alesea!" he shouted. I just kept running and never looked back.

"He was like a different person when he told me he never wanted to see Phoenix near me," I explained to Bernadet.

"Wow, you think he's jealous?" asked Bernadet.

After running out of school, I drove home and asked if the girls wanted to have a sleepover. Maeve said her house was not an option, so we went over to Bernadet's house.

"I don't know. Right now, I just want to avoid both of them."

"Good idea," said Maeve. "Boys are a pain anyway."

Bernadet and I laughed at Maeve's comment. Being around my best friends and having a sleepover, it was lovely. Nothing could ruin it.

Chapter 13

RYAN

Dammit, what is wrong with me? I just let my anger out on Alesea when I'm supposed to be making her like me. God, my dad's going to kill me.

After a long drive to the cabin, I went inside to tell my father what had happened.

"Young boss," greeted a member.

"Where's my father?"

He pointed to my father's room. I gave him a nod, a sign of *thank you*, and went to speak with my father. I knocked on the door—"Enter." I entered the room and closed the door. My father was staring out the window.

"Father," I greeted.

"Son," he greeted back.

He faced me. "I hope you made progress with the girl." I stayed quiet. "Ryan, you are making progress, yes?" he asked.

I cleared my throat. "I am. It's just . . . I made the mistake of scaring her."

My father, face still stone-cold, walked closer to me. "Explain to me how you scared her?" he asked. His voice was calm but I could tell that he was mad.

"I caught her making out with Phoenix, and my anger got the best of me."

His fist struck my face. "You idiot!" he shouted. "We need that girl to destroy the American Mafia."

My family is the Irish Mafia, and my dad has despised the American Mafia for years, ever since they attacked us years ago and killed my mother. I'll never forget that night.

"I understand, Father."

"Good boy. Now, tell me, what is this girl afraid of?" he asked.

I got up from the floor and told him what I had found out.

Chapter 14

ALESEA

The sleepover with the girls was very relaxing. It helped me get over Ryan's attitude and the incredible kiss I had with Phoenix.

At school, as I was getting my economics textbook, I turned and saw Ryan, holding my favorite flowers: daisies. I took them from him.

"I'm sorry for the way I acted. Can you forgive me?"

I held the flowers to my chest, smiling. "I forgive you."

He smiled and hugged me without ruining the flowers. "By the way, my father wants you to have dinner with us." He kissed my cheek.

"Sec you there."

Having dinner at my boyfriend's house and meeting his dad—what can go wrong?

Going through my closet, I couldn't find the perfect dining wear. Luckily, I found a dress that I was keeping in my closet for a special occasion. The dress used to be a plain, white, knee-length dress but, in art class, we mixed our clothes in dye. Now the dress was mixed with maroon, pink, and purple. After freshening up, I put on a little makeup and baked some pastries.

Putting Ryan's address into my car's GPS, I made it there without getting into traffic. Walking up to their doorstep, I noticed that their house was far from the road. It was strange.

I was about to ring the doorbell when a man—my guess was that he was in his thirties—opened the door.

"Ah, you must be Alesea." He held out his hand to me. "I'm Aiden, Ryan's father."

I shook his hand. "Nice to meet you, Mr. Saxfield."

"Please, call me Aiden."

"Well, nice to meet you, Aiden."

"Please come in. Dinner is almost ready."

The inside of their home was beautiful, the furniture was lovely, and the kitchen was gorgeous.

"I hope you don't mind—Ryan and I are half-Irish, so we wanted you to try our type of food."

The food may be different, but it's okay to try new things. "I don't mind, as long as you guys don't mind cream-filled pastries."

Ryan poked his head out of the kitchen. "I don't mind." He kissed my cheek. "You know I love your sweets."

Aiden started laughing at us: "All right, let's not let this good food go to waste."

Dinner was great. I'd never eaten lamb before. It was terrific, the shrimp and grits were flavorful, and the spinach-artichoke baked potatoes were delicious.

"Well, I must say, Aiden, this is the best Irish dinner I've ever had."

"Why thank you, Alesea. And I must say your cream-filled pastries were lovely." I was flattered by his compliment. Ryan got up from the table. "I hope you saved room for our dessert, Alesea." He went to the freezer and brought back three cups of ice cream. "I present to you: Guinness ice cream."

"Wow, it looks yummy."

Aiden picked up his ice cream. "Can't judge till you try it."

He took a bite from his spoon, then Ryan did from his, and then they both looked at me, waiting for me to try it. I took a spoonful, and it felt like my taste buds went to heaven.

"Wow, this is delicious," I said, with my mouth full.

"Told you she'd like it, Dad."

I did like it. I couldn't stop eating it. After we finished eating, I helped Ryan with the dishes.

"So, what did you think of my dad?" he asked.

"Your dad's nice."

A tiny smile formed on his lips. "Yeah. Yeah, he is." I tried to put up the dishes but, for some reason, I felt dizzy.

"Alesea, you okay?" Ryan asked.

I touched my forehead. "I'm okay, just a little tired." I almost lost my balance. Ryan caught me in his arms.

"Here, you should lie down." When my body landed onto the couch, my eyes started to grow heavy. Ryan put his hand on my cheek. "Sorry, Alesea, don't take this personally. But you were never my type."

My eyes were still so heavy, along with my body, but I forced them open. Getting up slowly, I looked around. I was in an underground room. *What had happened to me?* Memories from the dinner started coming back. I had had dinner with Ryan and his father, then Ryan gave his dad and me some ice cream, and after that I started feeling dizzy. *Did they drug me?*

The door creaked open and Ryan and his father Aiden walked in.

"Good morning, Alesea," Aiden greeted.

Anger, fear, and betrayal were all I felt toward them. "Y-you drugged me!"

"You catch on," said Ryan.

"Why?" I asked.

I was so confused. I hadn't done anything. Aiden walked closer to me and sat down. "You see, Alesea, we don't have anything against you. It's your parents we dislike."

My parents?

"W-what do Aaliyah and Emory have to do with this?"

"Not your adopted parents, Alesea. Your real parents."

Hayden and Madison?

"What do they have to do with me?"

Ryan walked closer to me, too. "They took someone important to us." I looked into his eyes and saw nothing but darkness. "My mother, Aili," he said. "Your parents attacked our mob years ago, and I was only three. My mother tried to keep me safe, but she died when she gave me to my dad. And we've blamed your parents since."

"Oh, my God. I'm so sorry."

Aiden put his hands on my shoulders. "Don't worry about it, dear, our revenge is just getting started. That's where you come in." He squeezed my shoulders harder. "Originally, you were supposed to die with your aunt and uncle years ago."

I was shocked. "You killed my aunt and uncle?"

He shrugged his shoulders. "Guilty as charged."

My blood was boiling. These two took away the people who took care of me. They were going to pay for what they'd done. He stood up from the bed.

"Anyway, now that we have you, we can get started. All we need to do is show them that we have you."

I was starting to get more nervous. "H-how, are you going to do that?"

Ryan smiled. It freaked me out.

"Not us—" he pointed at the door, "—him."

The door opened, and my fear increased to one-hundred percent.

"Y-you're supposed to be in jail."

He laughed at me. "Oh, baby, you know nothing can keep me away from you."

There he stood, with the disgusting smile on his face. Emory was here, and he wanted to hurt me again.

Chapter 15

PHOENIX

It was another day of Hell, better known as "school," and I hadn't seen Alesea or Saxfield. I noticed Bernadet and Maeve standing by their lockers, texting somebody. Must be Alesea. I walked up to them and asked, "Hey, you two seen Alesea?"

Maeve shook her head. "We haven't seen her or Ryan today."

"Maybe they're just sick," offered Bernadet. That was a possibility.

"Well, if you girls see her—" I took out a marker and wrote my number and their hands. "Give me a call."

A few days later, I was starting to get worried. No one had heard from Alesea for days, and I couldn't focus on anything else. Then my phone started ringing.

I answered, "Hello?"

"Phoenix, it's Maeve," she said.

"Yeah, what is it?"

"Can you come to Alesea's house? We know what happened to her."

"All right, I'm on my way."

I grabbed the keys to one of my cars and drove to her house as quickly as I could. When I arrived at her home I knocked on the door, hard. Ms. Macknight appeared behind the door.

"Thanks for coming, Phoenix," she said.

I entered her home. "No problem, Ms. Macknight. So, do you know what happened to Alesea?"

"Yes, but I think you should meet some people that I know." She showed me to the living room, and there I saw Bernadet and Maeve, a little girl, a young man, and two adults. "Phoenix, I want you to meet Alesea's real family." Ms. Macknight pointed to the two adults: "Her parents, Hayden and Madison Croft, and their children, Xavier and Maree."

I walked over to Mr. Croft and held out my hand. "It's nice to meet you, Mr. Croft."

He shook my hand. "Nice to meet you, too, Phoenix."

Then I shook his son's and wife's hands and patted the little one on the head.

"So, you said you know what happened to Alesea?"

"Yes," Mr. Croft answered. He gave me his phone. "This video was sent to us three days ago before we knew she was missing."

Aiden entered the video with a smug smile on his face. "Thought you'd never see me again, did ya? Well, as you can see, my son and I haven't forgotten what you did to our mob and my wife." The camera shifted and I saw Alesea, the clothes ripped right off her. She was shaking. "The first payback, the fire, didn't go so well, but this one will."

My blood was boiling, looking at Alesea.

"You don't look so good, Alesea. You want to tell them what happened?"

She looked into the camera, her eyes all puffy: "Emory's out of jail, an-and h-he touched me again."

She started crying, and the camera shifted back to Aiden.

"Such a shame. But don't worry, he's coming back for round two real soon." He then looked at the camera seriously. "Say bye-bye to your daughter, cause she belongs to us now."

The video ended.

"So, what do we do now?"

Mr. Croft stood up and stood right in front of me. "We know you're the best drug dealer here, and that you have a lot of men." He held out his hand. "Will you join our mob and rescue my daughter?"

I only had one answer to that question: "Yes." And, at that moment, my life was about to change.

Six months later, we found one of the Irish mob's hideouts and infiltrated it. We killed every member. Xavier and I went down into the basement, looking for Alesea.

"Hey, Phoenix, I found her."

I followed his voice to a door in the cellar. I entered and I couldn't believe my eyes.

"OH. MY. GOD."

I saw her with bruises on her face, but that's not what shocked me. What shocked me was her belly. Alesea was pregnant.

Chapter 16

I knew we couldn't just stand here. The place was about to fall.

"Come on. Grab your sister and let's go."

Xavier snapped out of it and grabbed his sister. We ran as fast as we could and called one of the men to get us to the closest hospital. When we got there, the doctors took Alesea and examined us. We only had a few cuts, but we still had to listen to the doctors.

"Does anything else hurt?" the doctor asked.

"No, we're good," Xavier said.

"All right, we'll have updates on your sister soon."

The doctor left us alone.

"We found her. After six months, we finally found her." Xavier said.

"Yeah, but you know we have to tell the others about . . ."

"I know. Her pregnancy."

He took out his phone and called his father. "Hey, Dad, it's me. Yeah, I'm okay." I heard Hayden crying on the other line. "There's just one problem." He took a deep breath. "Alesea's pregnant."

His dad cursed and hung up. He let out a deep sigh.

"Hey, come on, man." I put my hand on his shoulder. "We found her. That's all that matters."

He pinched his nose. "I know, it's just—I want to kill that asshole for putting his hands on her."

I nodded. "I know. So do I."

After waiting for two hours, his family arrived.

"Xavier, Phoenix, you guys okay?" Maeve asked.

Xavier softly kissed Maeve's lips. "We're fine, babe."

I'm glad he found happiness after his sister got kidnapped.

"Where's Alesea?" asked Madison.

"Second floor, room 253," the doctor said

We followed them to the room. When we got there, we were so nervous, but we knew we had to go in. I turned the doorknob and we all entered the room.

We saw a mask on Alesea's face. She was breathing, but that's not what caught everyone's attention. Their attention was on her pregnant belly.

"I-I can't believe this," Madison said.

She had the right to be shocked. Madison was anxious about her. Hayden was fuming with anger, but he held his wife in comfort. A doctor entered the room.

"Which of you are the parents?" she asked.

"We are," Hayden answered.

"Well, anyone who is not family has to wait outside."

I didn't want to leave Alesea, but I knew they would force me to go, so Maeve and I left the room. I didn't know what the doctor was telling them, but I was starting to get impatient.

The door opened, and the doctor came out.

"You and the family will have to leave soon, only one of you can stay."

"Thanks, doc."

We went back inside the room. Everyone was standing around Alesea's bed.

"What did the doctor say?" I asked.

"She clarified that there were only bruises on her face, not her body," explained Hayden.

"And since they got the smoke out of her lungs, she was lucky to survive. So was the baby," illustrated Xavier.

"Xavier and I are gonna go back to the house and interrogate the prisoners," disclosed Hayden. He looked at his wife. "Honey, you should go home with Maeve and rest." He looked at me seriously. "Phoenix, you helped us find our daughter, and we trust you." He walked over to me and put both hands on my shoulders. "Will you stay and watch her?"

He didn't even have to ask me. "Hayden, I've worked for you for six months. You've taught me everything about raising my business. I will not leave your daughter's side, no matter what."

He gave me a side hug. "Thank you."

So, they left the hospital and left me alone with Alesea. I took a seat right next to her bed and looked at her.

"Alesea, I don't know if you can hear me, but I promise you I'll find those bastards and make them pay." I took hold of her hand. "And, for the past six months I haven't been able to tell you, but I think now would be the best time: I love you, Alesea."

I got up from my seat and kissed her forehead. I sat back down and felt a little squeeze on my hand. I looked at her; she was smiling. Then she started coughing, so I rang for the nurse.

Chapter 17

The nurses came by and checked her blood pressure, took the oxygen mask off her, and checked her heartbeat. When they finally left, I called Alesea's parents, and they said that they were on their way. While we were waiting for them, I tried talking to her, but she just stayed quiet. I took her hand.

"Hey?"

She looked at me, and her face and her eyes showed no emotion.

"Did you hear what I said?"

She nodded her head.

I smiled and took hold of both of her hands. "I promise you, Alesea, even if the child isn't mine, I'll support your decision to keep the baby or get an abortion."

She shook her head. "I'm keeping the baby," she whispered.

I was confused. "But why, why keep this bastard's child?"

"Because this baby didn't do anything wrong. Plus, Aaliyah deserves to be the godmother," she explained.

This woman, who was right in front of me, has the biggest heart of anyone I've ever met.

We heard the door open and her family and Maeve entered the room. I figured this was their time to be alone with their daughter.

"Hey, Maeve, can I talk to you outside?" I asked.

She looked at Xavier, he nodded firmly, and she followed me out the door. "What is it?" Maeve asked.

This news was going to shock her, but not as much as it's going to shock her parents. I took a deep breath.

"Alesea wants to keep the baby."

"W-why would she want to keep that pervert's baby?!"

I explained to her everything Alesea had told me and she understood, I guess.

The door burst open. Hayden stormed out of the room; Madison went after him. We walked back into the room and Alesea was staring at the ceiling, tears running down her face.

"What happened?" Maeve asked.

Xavier pinched his nose and let out a deep sigh. "Our dad got upset that she said that she was gonna keep the baby." He took hold of her hand. "I'm so sorry, Alesea."

She squeezed his hand back.

Xavier put his hand on Maeve's shoulder. "Hey, babe, would you mind staying with her? I don't think she needs to be alone right now."

She nodded and kissed his cheek. "I'll see you tomorrow."

He kissed her back. "Night, sweetheart." He kissed Alesea's cheek. "Night, Alesea. I love you."

She replied, "I love you, too."

He left the room, waiting for me to follow. Before I could go, I hugged Maeve and kissed Alesea's forehead.

"I love you."

She smiled and replied, "I love you, too."

Chapter 18

ALESEA

I tried to get some sleep, but my mind went back to that underground basement. I'll never forget what Emory did to me for six months.

Six months ago, the moment my eyes laid on Emory, the color drained from my face, and I felt sick. The moment Ryan and Saxfield left us alone, he came towards me and took advantage of me.

Every morning a servant would bring me breakfast. I refused the meal every time. It upset Aiden that I wouldn't eat. He told me that if I refused to eat, he would punish me. So, I refused to eat both breakfast and lunch.

For some reason, it made Emory sad. I thought he was going to force himself onto me as usual, but I was so wrong. When he came back, my eyes caught sight of the whip in his hand. I was so frightened this was my new punishment, and I didn't like it.

He kept beating me and beating me until I started shaking. He told me that if I kept refusing to eat, the whip would be my new punishment; I had no choice but to obey.

It was like this every day: I had breakfast, and Emory took advantage of me.

A month later, or so I thought, I started feeling sick. Every time I ate breakfast, I puked it out, and I felt more tired than before. I was hoping I wasn't pregnant because if I were, I would kill myself. Ryan noticed how sick I was feeling. He called the mob doctor and tested me. I was traumatized by his response.

"Ms. Macknight, you're pregnant."

Emory found out the moment the mob doctor left. He was overjoyed. He was finally going to have a child of his own. They added extra security to my "room," making sure I didn't kill myself and the baby.

I had to get out of there. My child could not live like this.

For a few weeks, I played nice, and they fell for the act. My bump was getting bigger every day. Emory finally let me out of that awful basement and put me in a room, filled with nursery items. His bedroom was right across from mine. The more I kept the act up, the more I was able to go outside and look around for my escape plan.

I noticed two guards blocking a path to the forest, which gave me an idea for my escape.

I waited a few more days to put my plan into action.

Nighttime finally came. I put on some clothes and made sure no one was at my door. I completed phase one of my escape, but I wasn't out of the woods yet. As I got outside, I saw the guards in the same spot, blocking my way out. I hid behind a tree, looking for something that would attract their attention. My foot found a rock and an idea came to mind. Picking up the stone, I threw it as far as I could to the left, hitting a bush.

"What was that?" asked the guard from the left.

"I don't know. Let's check it out," followed the guard from the right.

The guards followed the sound and left the woods unguarded. I took my chance and ran, knowing that it hurt my abdomen. I thought I was finally free, but then I heard a loud siren. I ran faster. I heard footsteps following me, so I picked up the pace. I saw a street up ahead and ran like crazy.

I made it to the street, but a black car stopped right in front of me. The door opened and Emory came out with an enraged look. "You are in so much trouble, Alesea." He brought his fist to my face, knocking me out.

My head was pounding so much. I tried to move, but I felt my hands bound to something. I opened my eyes, seeing everything in a blur. After a few more seconds, my eyesight started to come back. I saw Emory staring right at me.

He let out a tired sigh. "Oh, Alesea, I thought we were going to be happy." He came over and touched my belly. "I mean, you're carrying my child, for God's sake." He started circling me. "But you just had to be your stubborn self and run away." He walked away from me and picked up an object from the bed. My face went pale at the object in his hand: a knife. He sighed again. "Sorry, love, but you brought this on yourself." He turned me around, cut my shirt.

"Please, please, Emory."

"You should've thought about that before you ran away."

I didn't want to scream but the knife on my back was unbearable. The tears were coming down but I didn't want him to hear me.

"Alesea! Alesea!"

I woke up. My body was sweating.

"It's okay, Alesea. It's was just a nightmare." Maeve comforted me and talked to me until I fell back asleep. That night, I was able to sleep without thinking about the last six months.

Chapter 19

The hospital let me go after a few more days of checking my blood sugar and the baby. My parents picked me up and drove me to their house. It was a long drive, but my family was there to comfort me. I was silent for the whole ride. I didn't know what to say. Also, my dad was still upset with me for saying that I was going to keep the baby.

Maree tried lightening up the mood by putting on a kiddie song. It did lighten up the mood just a bit— Xavier even recorded Dad singing and posted it on Snapchat. That made me smile just a little.

After hours of driving and stopping for gas, we finally made it back to the mansion. Xavier and Dad carried my stuff to what was supposed to have been my room, which they had now renovated. Xavier sat down on the left side of the bed.

"Mom bought you some maternity clothes to wear." He pointed at the closet.

I nodded. He kissed my forehead and left Dad and me alone. I figured he didn't want to talk to me, so I lay down. He sighed and sat on my bed.

"I'm not mad at you, honey," he explained. "I was just surprised that you wanted to keep that bastard's child."

"This baby is innocent. He or she did nothing wrong," I told him.

"I know, and I'm proud of you for making that decision. Just know that I will always love you."

For weeks I'd been in my room, doing nothing but staring at the ceiling. Sometimes my family would come and try to talk to me. It only worked for a little bit.

I ate dinner with them, and Phoenix came over sometimes, as well. Phoenix and I were growing closer than ever; he said he would help me through the pregnancy. My friends came over and looked after me, as well, from time to time. Maeve told us that she and Xavier were expecting. I was so excited: not only was I going to be an aunt, my child was going to have a cousin.

After staying in the house for so long, I decided one day that it was time for me to get out. Luckily, I had an ultrasound that day, so I asked Phoenix to come with me.

We arrived at the clinic and the doctor came in and greeted us, "Hi, I'm Dr. Bachelor. You must be Alesea." He shook my hand and Phoenix's.

"Yes, that's me, and this is Phoenix, my boyfriend." My heart fluttered when I said the word *boyfriend*.

"Well, first, congratulations. Let's get started."

Dr. Bachelor was very relaxing to be around. I was sure he'd done this many times before. When he started rubbing the tool on my gelled stomach, the monitor came on, showing the inside of my abdomen.

"Well, I see the head, and the baby looks pretty healthy." I looked over at Phoenix and saw him smiling at the ultrasound of the baby. "Would you like to know the gender?" asked Dr. Bachelor.

"Yes, please," said Phoenix.

The doctor moved the handle more down and told us, "It's a girl."

When he told us that I was having a girl, I felt the tears coming down. Then Dr. Bachelor moved the handle over to the other side of my stomach, and the monitor showed another baby's head.

"And that's a boy. You're having twins!" he explained.

Twins? I'm having twins!

Chapter 20

After we left the clinic, we both couldn't let the excitement go. *I was carrying twins!* And I already knew I was going to name them after my deceased parents: Mikey Junior, or MJ, and Allie. I know my mom and dad would be pleased about the names.

While we were driving back to my place, I had to ask Phoenix a question that had been bugging me: "Any leads on Emory and the Irish mob?"

Phoenix chuckled a little. "You sounded like a mobster, asking me that."

"I'm a mobster's daughter, Phoenix."

He chuckled again. "But, to answer your question: We do have a lead."

"What'd you find out?"

"We noticed that one of our crew members has been acting strangely, so Xavier and I have been keeping tabs on him. His name is Deortun. You've probably seen him around."

I'd seen him around the mansion and I'd always had this weird feeling about him. Sometimes I caught him around my room.

"When you went out of the house with your friends, Xavier went into your room and found bugs."

"What?!"

I was so shocked that traitor bugged my room.

"We've checked every inch of the house for more bugs, and we figured that Deortun was a mole and working with the Irish mob." I felt anger swell up inside me. *How could someone betray my family?* "We tried looking for him around the mansion, but it seems he's disappeared." Phoenix took his hand from the wheel and put it over mine. "Don't worry, Alesea. We'll protect you."

I started to relax, knowing that I have people who love me and protect me from danger.

I noticed that we had passed my street a few miles back.

"Phoenix, you know we missed our turn, right?" He nodded. "Where are we going?"

He smiled. "It's a surprise." He continued driving to this "surprise" he had for me. "Okay, we're almost there, but I want you to cover your eyes." I raised my eyebrow. "It'll ruin the surprise, Alesea." I sighed and covered my eyes.

Phoenix continued driving, then parked the car. I heard him get out of the car and open my side of the vehicle.

"Give me your hand, but keep your eyes covered."

I reached out for his hand and he pulled me forward.

Phoenix stopped and said, "Okay, you can uncover your eyes now."

Removing my hands, I saw the most beautiful two-story house I'd ever seen.

"Phoenix, what is this?"

He stood in front of me and kissed my lips. "This, my dear, is our house."

Phoenix gave me a tour of the house. Every room except for the bedroom across from the master bedroom had furniture. That was meant to be the twins' room. The kitchen was so shiny, with black counters with white marble tops. The master bathroom was enormous:

the bathtub was large enough to fit two and the shower had two faucets.

Finally, he showed me the backyard. We had one of those pools from Pool Kings—the deck was like a spa, with a hot tub and a waterfall at the end. Phoenix lead me to the fire pit.

"So, what do you think?" he asked.

I kissed him. "I love it."

He smiled at me. "I knew you would."

I felt something hard hit my stomach. Phoenix looked concerned. "What's wrong?" The look on his face made me laugh.

"I think one of the twins started kicking."

His eyes lit up; he put his hand on my stomach. "MJ, is that you?"

There was another kick, which meant that Mikey was the one kicking.

"I think that's a yes." He kissed my tummy and said, "Daddy can't wait to see you and your sister." There was a light kick in my belly, meaning Allie was listening, too. He kissed my tummy again and then kissed me. "Ready to try out the bed?"

I nodded, and he led me right back to our room.

Chapter 21

After staying the night at our new house, we decided that once we moved in we'd have a house party-slash-baby shower and tell everyone the babies' genders. My dad mentioned to me that he and Xavier would be out, following a lead on Deotrun. So, it was just Maree and me with some guards.

We were playing with Maree's toys in her room when, suddenly, we heard gunshots around the house. Maree got scared and started crying. I held her close, protecting her and the twins. One of the guards barged into the room: "Hurry! The Irish mob is attacking us!"

My anxiety picked up. It meant that Emory was here, too.

I picked up Maree and followed the guard, away from the gunfire. For some reason, I had a bad feeling in my gut.

"Um, excuse me, but where are we going?" I asked.

"There's a road on the other side of these woods. There's a car waiting for you and your sister," he explained.

I trusted him, but I still had a bad feeling in my stomach. When I saw the road up ahead, the bad taste in my mouth increased, but what I saw later made it worse. Aiden and Emory came out of the car with smug smiles on their faces.

"Hello, Alesea, did you miss me?" asked Emory.

I tried to run, but before I could even run, I felt someone snatch my sister out of my hands and gag me. My vision started to blur while I heard Maree screaming my name. After that, I heard nothing and saw nothing but darkness.

****

PHOENIX

When I dropped Alesea back at her parents' house, I called up some interior designers to paint our house while I went shopping for something important. I drove to Gold and Gods, the jewelry store, to find the perfect ring for Alesea. I entered the store and walked over to a female employee, Ashlee, in the ring section.

"Hello, sir. Welcome to Gold and Gods. How can I help you?"

"I'm looking for an engagement ring for my girlfriend."

"Well, sir, today is your lucky day. We happened to receive a new engagement ring today," she explained. "I can show you if you'd like?"

I nodded.

Ashlee took me to the engagement ring section and pulled out a ring with a bunch of diamonds around a gold ring. "Now, this just came in this week. This is the eternity ring. It shows that you'll want to be with the woman you love for the rest of your life," she explained.

The ring looked perfect.

"I'll take it."

Ashlee rang me up and put the ring into a black ring container. "Nice choice, sir, and good luck."

While driving back to the manor, my phone started ringing.

"Hello?"

"Phoenix, it's me," answered Xavier.

"What is it, man?"

"The lead we found was a fake, and I just got a call from one of our men saying the Irish mob attacked us. And what's worse, Alesea and Maree are missing."

My blood was boiling. I felt like I was going to explode.

"I'm on my way."

I sped through traffic to get to the manor. When I arrived, I saw bullet holes through the windows and some bodies inside and outside of the estate. I found Xavier and Hayden by a road far away from the manor.

"Any leads?" I asked them.

"Only one." Hayden showed me Alesea's phone.

"We found it out by the road, and I think we can use her phone to our advantage."

"How?"

"You see, Phoenix, we gave my little sister a burner phone to use just for emergencies. And she never leaves without it. So, in case of an emergency, we gave her Alesea's number along with ours," explained Xavier.

We heard a ding come from the phone.

"This is Maree's number," explained Hayden.

The phone showed a text: *At an old abandoned factory. Took sissy away.*

"There's a factory that's only two miles away from here. It's been abandoned for years," explained Xavier.

"Well, we know where we are heading," said Hayden.

We suited up for battle and headed straight to the factory.

Hang on, Alesea. We're coming, I told myself.

Chapter 22

ALESEA

My head was pounding as if someone had hit me in the head with the back of a gun. Opening my eyes, my vision was starting to become more apparent. I looked up and saw other men standing around me. Memorics of what had happened started coming back, that Emory and Saxfield had kidnapped Maree and me. I tried to move my hands, but they were tied behind the chair I was sitting in.

"Hey, boss, she's up," one of the men shouted.

Footsteps were coming towards me. The men separated, and Aiden and Ryan stood right in front of me. Aiden looked at his men. "Leave us," he ordered.

His men nodded and left us alone. Aiden took a knee and smiled at me, smugly. "How you been, Alesea?" I glared at him, showing that he didn't scare me. "Silent treatment, huh? That's all right, you don't have to talk." He put his hand on the chair. "Just listen." My blood was boiling so severely, but I had to stay calm for the twins. Then I remembered Maree.

"Where's my sister?!"

"Oh, little Maree. She's fine. A biter, too," Aiden explained, rubbing his hand.

"You know you won't . . ."

"Oh, but my dear, we already have," Aiden interrupted. "You see, with you and your sister with us, your family will have no choice but to come to your rescue. And when they do, my team will strike," he explained.

My blood went cold as ice. *My family won't be able to see what they're planning.*

"Ryan, take her to her sister." Ryan came behind me with a pocket knife, releasing me.

He led me to a room where I heard crying. Ryan unlocked the door and I saw Maree crying on the run-down bed. "Maree!" When she saw me, she ran into my arms and hugged me tightly.

"You okay? Did they hurt you?"

"She's fine, I made sure of it," Ryan interrupted. Those were the first words he ever said to me. He was about to leave, but he stopped mid-way. "Alesea, don't try to escape. If you do, they'll kill Maree."

Chapter 23

Maree and I had been waiting in that awful room for an hour. If I left, they'd kill her. I was so confused; I didn't know what to do. Then I saw a window that was the same size as Maree.

"Maree, I got an idea," I whispered.

"What?" she asked.

I pointed to the window. "You see that window?" She nodded. "I'm gonna give you a boost, and you're gonna escape through the window and see if you can find some help. Okay?"

She looked at the window again. "Okay."

I gave Maree a boost up, without hurting the twins, and pushed her through the window. She hit the ground with a soft thud. I stood on the bed and looked. Maree was standing outside the factory. "Good girl. Now, go find help, and stay hidden."

She nodded and ran away from the window.

****

MAREE

I ran and ran as fast as I could. If I heard people coming, I hid behind a tree or stayed low in the tall grass. I could see the road up ahead. I ran faster, but I felt someone grab my wrist. Two big men stared at me.

"Well, well, well. Looks like we got a stowaway," one of the big men stated. My daddy always taught me that size doesn't matter, so I kicked the man who was holding my wrist in the face. And took a stick and hit him in the head. The other man was about to grab me, but I was faster. Going under his legs, I kicked his kneecap, making him fall on the ground and hitting him in the head with the same stick. Both men were on the ground.

I heard clapping behind me. I thought it was another enemy. I turned, and it wasn't an enemy I saw, it was my daddy. "Daddy!" I ran and jumped into his arms, giving him a big hug.

"We were so worried about you, sweet pea."

Then Xavier came over and patted my head. "You were so brave."

I smiled. "Thanks, brother."

Next, Phoenix came over, looking severe.

"Where's your sister?"

I pointed to the factory.

"All right," said Daddy. He gave me to one of the bodyguards—"Take her to the car and make sure she stays there."

The guard nodded. "Yes, sir."

My daddy was about to leave with the rest of the guards, Xavier and Phoenix.

"Daddy!" I shouted. He looked at me. I was on the verge of tears, but I held them back. "I love you."

He smiled at me. "I love you, too, sweet pea."

Chapter 24

ALESEA

After I helped Maree out the window, I was just standing on the bed, waiting. While waiting, I was starting to have pains in my abdomen. Either they were from something I had eaten or . . . *no, no, no, no. I can't be having the twins now, it's not even my due date yet.*

The door opened and Emory entered, carrying a tray of food. "I brought you some— . . . Where's your sister?" he asked. "Dammit, Alesea, why do you have to be so stubborn!"

I got up from the bed, clutching my stomach. "I'm stubborn. I'm trying to survive this battle with the Saxfields and protect my children!"

He was about to slap me, but I grabbed his wrist and punched him in the nose. He held his nose and looked at me.

"You've changed," he said.

"I'm not the same girl that you took advantage of."

I felt something wet touch my feet. I looked down and saw water coming out of my pants.

"Oh, no." I looked at Emory, and he had an enormous smile on his face.

"Oh, yes." He looked back at me. "I'm finally gonna be a dad."

When my water broke, I was more scared than excited. The twins were coming at the wrong time. After Emory saw the water on the floor, he planned to drag me to the hospital so that he could see his kids' birth. The hallway was cleared; he started pulling me to the exit.

"Don't fight me, Alesea," he said, looking at me with a smug smile. "We don't want you to have the twins here now, do we?"

I glared at him while he continued to drag me along.

Suddenly, gunshots surrounded the building.

"We're being apprehended!" The excitement was coursing through my veins. They had found me.

"Shit, come on." Dragging me more roughly, we finally made it outside. "Come on, get in."

Emory put me inside the car and locked me inside. But before he could open the door, a bullet hit his shoulder, causing blood to splatter and a bullet hole in the window. I looked and saw Phoenix with a gun in his hand. He saw me and smiled. I tried to smile back, but I was caught by a scream from the contraction I was having.

Two of our members got me into the car. "Don't worry, princess, we'll get you to the hospital."

I was relieved my babies were going to be born in a hospital.

Chapter 25

When we arrived at the hospital, the contractions were getting worse and worse.

"I'll stay outside and keep a look out. You take the princess and make sure she delivers safely," the driver said.

"Alright," answered another member. He opened my door and took me straight to the entrance. "We need a doctor!" he shouted.

A female nurse came by with a wheelchair. "What's the problem?" she asked.

"She's in labor," he explained.

"Are you the father?" asked the nurse.

I know she's just doing her job, but I'm in pain here!

"No, I work for the father."

The nurse nodded and led me to the labor room. Since the babies were close to coming, the doctor suggested I have a C-section. And it was successful.

There I was, in my room, holding my beautiful babies. My little angels. The door opened, revealing Phoenix.

"Are you okay?" he asked, looking worried.

"*Shhh.*" The twins were asleep, and I didn't want them to be woken up. "I'm fine."

He saw the twins in my arms, and a smile appeared on his face. He came over to my bed, looking at the kids' beautiful faces. "They're adorable." MJ opened his eyes and looked at Phoenix. "Hey, buddy."

"You wanna hold him?"

He nodded. I let him gently take MJ out of my left arm. "He's handsome." He looked at Allie. "And she's beautiful." There was a knock on the door, and my family entered the room with smiles on their faces and tears down their eyes. I gave Allie to my mom. She had tears running down her face.

"Oh, Alesea, you made such wonderful children."

"Thanks, Mom."

She was right, I did make beautiful children. And now I'm happy.

****

PHOENIX

After the men took Alesea to the hospital, I held my gun high at this pervert. He just stood there with a smug smile.

"What are you gonna do now, boy? You gonna kill me?"

I shrugged. "As fun as that would sound, I not gonna kill you." I put the gun away. "I'm just gonna beat the holy hell out of you."

I threw the first punch, which knocked him to the ground. He got up and tried to punch me in the face, but I dodged it, hitting his left cheek. Putting him on the ground again, I kicked him in the stomach, making him cough up blood. I kicked him continuously as he held his stomach tightly. I grabbed his hair, making him face me. "Apologize." With his messed-up face looking at me, he looked confused. "Apologize for what you did."

"I—I, I . . ." he tried to answer, "I loved it."

That pissed me off so badly, but I was gonna let Xavier and Hayden take care of the more significant ass-beating. So I just knocked him out. I entered the factory, dragging that old bastard, and the only men I saw standing were Xavier, Hayden, the Saxfields, and some of the crew members. I kept dragging Emory over to the Saxfields because he'd be joining them in Hell.

"I see you brought the man of the hour," Hayden said.

I dropped him next to Ryan. "Yeah, but he said something horrible about your daughter." I saw the anger on both Hayden's and Xavier's faces.

"What he'd say?" asked Xavier.

I looked at Emory with an evil smile across my face, making him go pale. "He said he enjoyed every bit of your daughter."

Hayden looked at Emory like he was going to cut him into tiny pieces. I believed he would.

"You go to the hospital. We'll deal with these pigs," he said.

"You sure you don't want me to stay?"

Xavier put his hand on my shoulder. "Go, my sister needs you right now. Besides," he looked back at the Saxfields and at Emory, "I'm gonna enjoy this." I nodded and left them to have all the fun.

When I finally arrived at the hospital, I found Alesea's room, where she had already finished giving birth.

"Are you okay?" I asked, worried.

She replied that she was okay. When I saw the twins in her arms, I was so happy. I knew they weren't biologically mine, but I planned to treat MJ and Allie as if they were my own.

Chapter 26

ALESEA

The moment Phoenix and I took the twins to our new home, we realized that being a parent is a hard job. And with twins, it's double crying, double diapers, and double hunger. But Phoenix and I had a little help from my parents.

The twins were lovely to each other and to their family, but MJ and Allie have different personalities. MJ was a very inquisitive toddler. He liked to get into things like the kitchen cabinets, the cleaning cabinets, and the silverware drawer. We had to baby-proof the house. Allie was an independent toddler. She was figuring things out herself and she hated it when we tried to help her with something, even if she needed it.

While I had been at home watching the twins, Phoenix had decided to leave the drug dealing to his best friend and focus starting his own business.

We weren't the only ones who changed in the months after the twins' birth. Like my mom and dad: They were now the king and queen of all mafias. If anybody double-crossed them, you'd know what happens. And my brother and Maeve got married and had a baby girl, Marcee.

After having the twins and becoming an aunt, my life couldn't get any better. Or so I thought.

I was in the twins' room one day, teaching them how to talk. They're brilliant. I was trying to get one of them to say *mama* instead of *dada*. A knock on the door interrupted my teaching. "Come in." Phoenix entered the room.

"Hey," he greeted.

"Hey."

Allie crawled to Phoenix. "Hey, princess." He picked her up and kissed her cheek.

"Hey, baby, what are you doing tonight?" he asked.

"I don't think I have any plans tonight."

"Great. Dress nicely, I have something special planned for us."

"Okay."

I called Xavier and Maeve to watch the twins, so Marcee could play with her cousins. I put on a knee-length dress that covered my back and arms. The doorbell rang. I let Xavier, Maeve, and Marcee inside.

"Hey guys, the twins are in the living room." The twins were excited to see their uncle, aunt, and cousin. "We'll be back in an hour or so." We kissed the twins goodbye and left for our date.

Phoenix took me to our favorite Italian restaurant. He ordered soup and shrimp fettuccine alfredo for me, and he got the make-your-own pasta meal. After we had our dinner, he took me to a five- star hotel and got us a lovers' suite.

Upon entering the lovers' suite, I saw that rose petals were leading to the balcony. The balcony had a table with champagne flutes, a bottle of champagne, and a little box.

"Phoenix, what is all this?" I asked curiously.

"Well, you know that I was a real player a year ago, but I still tried to get your attention. And now that we have the twins, you and the kids are the only things I want to focus on." He picked up the little box from the table. *Hold on—a romantic dinner, a lovers' suite, and a small container could mean only one thing . . .*

He got on one knee. "Alesea, after trying to get your attention since senior year, going through your pregnancy, and becoming parents, I realized that you're the one I want to be with for the rest of my life." He opened the box, revealing the most beautiful ring I'd ever seen. "Alesea, will you make me the happiest man on earth and marry me?"

Tears came streaming down my face. "Yes, yes!"

"I love you so much," he said.

"I love you, too, Phoenix."

We ended up talking about wedding planning while drinking champagne and having fun in the suite.

Chapter 27

After seven months of planning our wedding, the day had finally come. The day I was going to become Mrs. Lazaro.

I was in my dressing room, with my mom and my best friends helping me with my dress, makeup, and hair. The gown was a Pnina Tornai: an A-line off-the-shoulder dress with a corset bodice, long sleeves, and embroidered skirt. I had been surprised, live, to be on *Say Yes to the Dress* and had met Randy Fenoli, too.

We had decided to have our wedding at the Palace of Arts Center in Grapevine, Texas. After my friends finished my makeup, a knock on the door interrupted their work in progress.

"Come in," answered Bernadet.

My dad entered the room. "It's time."

The girls finished the last touches of my makeup before they left. My dad came over and looked at me in the mirror.

"You look so beautiful, honey."

"Thanks, Dad."

"I got you something." He pulled out a black, velvet necklace box. "Close your eyes," he said.

I closed my eyes and something cold wrapped around my neck.

"Open your eyes."

I opened them, and I saw the most beautiful necklace I'd ever seen. It was a silver necklace with a heart figure that had a ruby inside of it.

"It was Allie's necklace. I figured she would have wanted you to have it."

I had to keep the tears in; I didn't want to ruin my makeup. I gave my dad a big hug. "Thanks, Dad. It's beautiful."

"You're welcome, sweetheart." We heard the music playing right outside the room. "You ready?"

I nodded. "As I'll ever be."

We left the room and my dad walked me down the aisle to my soon-to-be husband. Being by Phoenix's side, listening to the preacher, and reciting our vows was the most romantic thing that's ever happened to me.

"Phoenix, do you take Alesea to be your wife, to have and to hold, in sickness and in health, for as long as you shall live?" asked the preacher.

"I do."

"And Alesea, do you take Phoenix to be your husband, to have and to hold, in sickness and in health, for as long as you shall live?"

I couldn't hold them in anymore, the tears just came right out. "I do."

"Then, by the power vested in me by the state of Texas, I now pronounce you husband and wife. Phoenix you may—"

He didn't wait for the preacher to finish. He dipped me and kissed me right on the lips. "—do *that*."

We heard cheering and clapping, but that didn't matter to us. All that mattered was our new life together.

Epilogue

It's been eight years since Phoenix and I got married. After the wedding, we went to the Maldives, in Asia, for our honeymoon. We did some sightseeing, relaxed at the hotel, and banged, which got me pregnant again with our third child.

When we came back from our honeymoon, the twins were excited to have another sibling. MJ wanted a brother he could play with, while Allie wanted a sister she could dress up. Six months later, we found out we were having a boy. Phoenix was so happy. After we found out it was a boy, we decided to name him Loki.

After Loki was born, our family couldn't have been any more complete. I was finally happy. If my mom and dad were here, they would be so proud of me.

CPSIA information can be obtained
at www.ICGtesting.com
Printed in the USA
BVHW041551300120
570973BV00006B/631

9 781612 447902